EDGE
BOOKS

WARRIORS OF HISTORY

ZULU
WARRIORS

by Terri Dougherty

Consultant:
Atieno Adala
Managing Editor
Africa Today

Capstone
press

Mankato, Minnesota

Edge Books are published by Capstone Press,
151 Good Counsel Drive, P.O. Box 669, Mankato, Minnesota 56002.
www.capstonepress.com

Library of Congress Cataloging-in-Publication Data
Dougherty, Terri.
    Zulu warriors / by Terri Dougherty.
    p. cm. — (Edge books. Warriors of history)
    Includes bibliographical references and index.
    ISBN-13: 978-1-4296-1313-2 (hardcover)
    ISBN-10: 1-4296-1313-0 (hardcover)
    1. Zulu (African people) — Wars. 2. Zulu (African people) — History. 3.
Zulu (African people) — Government relations. 4. Zulu War, 1879. 5. Zululand
(South Africa) — History — To 1879. 6. Great Britain — Colonies — Africa.
I. Title. II. Series.
DT1768.Z95S54 2008
968'.0049639869 — dc22   2007029961

Summary: Describes the life of a Zulu warrior, including his training, weapons,
    and what led to the downfall of his society.

Editorial Credits
Mandy Robbins, editor; Kyle Grenz, book designer; Thomas Emery, set designer;
    Jo Miller, photo researcher; Tod Smith, illustrator; Krista Ward, colorist

Photo Credits
Art Resource, N.Y./HIP, 4, 12; Snark, 21
Corbis, 13; Hulton-Deutsh Collection, 24, 25; Michael Masian Historic
    Photographs, 6
Getty Images Inc./AFP/Alexander Joe, 29; Hulton Archive, 16, 22
Mary Evans Picture Library, 8–9, 14, 26–27; John Monck, cover, 10

1 2 3 4 5 6 13 12 11 10 09 08

TABLE OF CONTENTS

CHAPTER 1

FIERCE WARRIORS

LEARN ABOUT

- A stunning victory
- The Zulu nation
- Skilled warriors

The British were overwhelmed by the Zulu at Isandlwana Hill.

In January 1879, the Zulu and the British were fighting a fierce war in southern Africa. British forces set up camp at Isandlwana Hill. British Lieutenant General Lord Chelmsford thought he knew where the Zulu warriors were camped. He decided to move toward them and attack. He marched away with almost half the British forces.

Lieutenant Colonel Henry Pulleine stayed behind with 1,700 soldiers. A group of Pulleine's soldiers looked over a ridge and were completely shocked. Thousands of Zulu warriors were camped below them in the valley. Just then, the warriors saw the British. They rushed out of the valley, carrying deadly spears and clubs.

The British were taken by complete surprise. They tried to spread out their troops to stop the Zulu attack. But the Zulu sneaked past the British through the tall grass. The confident warriors rushed at the British from all sides.

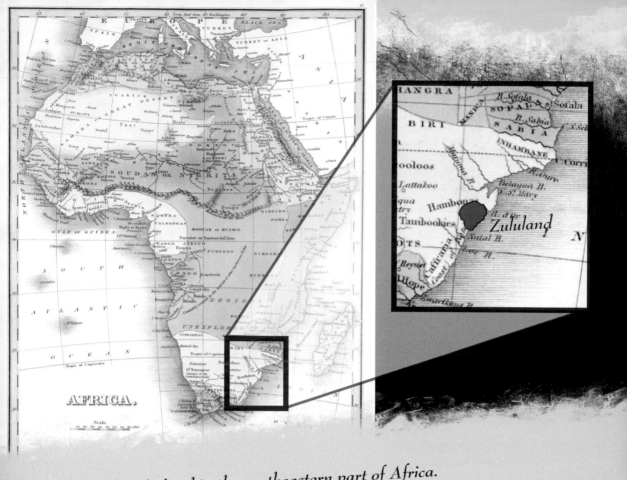

The Zulu lived in the southeastern part of Africa.
They called their country Zululand.

The British shot at the Zulu, while Zulu spears rained down on British troops. The Zulu drove the British back and raided their stock of guns. More than 1,000 British troops and 1,000 Zulu warriors were killed. Colonel Pulleine was among the dead.

ZULULAND

The Zulu people have lived in southeastern Africa since the 1500s. In the early 1800s, King Shaka led an army that conquered many other nations in the area. The Zulu went to war with other groups of people to control more land and defeat their enemies. At its peak, Zululand covered a large part of what is now South Africa.

Zulu kings held a great deal of power. Many of their own people plotted to take it from them. Shaka was stabbed by his brothers in 1828. The next Zulu king, Dingane, was also killed by his own people. Mpande then became the Zulu leader. In the late 1800s, Mpande's son Cetshwayo ruled the Zulu.

African nations were not the only people living near Zululand. By the mid-1800s, settlers from the Netherlands and Great Britain had come to Africa. They found diamonds, gold, and elephant tusks to sell. The Europeans also wanted to control the shipping route that went around Africa's coast. Fighting broke out as the settlers moved closer to Zulu territory.

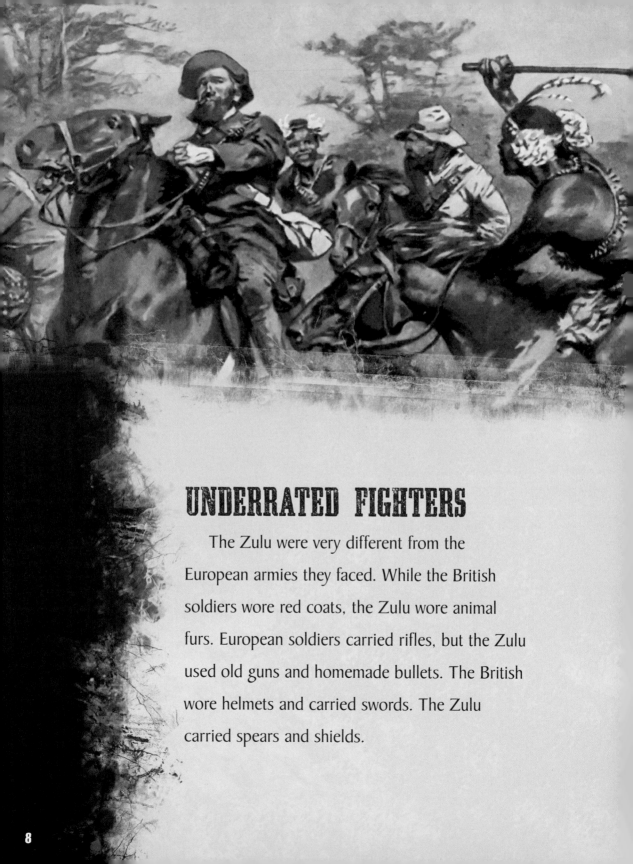

UNDERRATED FIGHTERS

The Zulu were very different from the European armies they faced. While the British soldiers wore red coats, the Zulu wore animal furs. European soldiers carried rifles, but the Zulu used old guns and homemade bullets. The British wore helmets and carried swords. The Zulu carried spears and shields.

The Dutch settlers in Africa who fought the Zulu were called the Boers.

Enemies thought the Zulu were ignorant and wild. But the Zulu army was quite organized, and its warriors were excellent spearmen. The Zulu also had the advantage of fighting in their own land. They knew how to move quickly across difficult ground. The Zulu seemed less advanced to other armies. But the skill of the Zulu warriors often surprised their enemies.

9

CHAPTER II

LIFE IN ZULULAND

LEARN ABOUT

- *Farmers and soldiers*
- *Zulu homes*
- *Serving the king*

The Zulu word for homestead is umuzi.

When the nation was not at war, Zulu men were farmers. They raised cattle in the grasslands of Africa. The more cattle a man had, the richer he was.

The Zulu people also raised crops. Women worked the soil, harvested grain, and cooked for their families. Men cared for the cattle, made tools for farming, and built homes.

Zulu homes were made of matted grass. These cone-shaped huts were cool in summer and warm in winter.

A homestead included a number of huts that sat in a circle. Family members lived in some of the huts. Other huts were used for storing vegetables and grain. A family's cattle grazed in the center of the ring. The Zulu people also held ceremonies in the center of the ring.

King Shaka was a fierce warrior.
His motto was "death or victory."

A POWERFUL KING

The Zulu king had power over the entire country, especially the army. He commanded the Zulu to go to war. When the nation was at peace, he had soldiers work his land for him. The king also told his soldiers when they could get married. They had to marry women who were born in a certain year. Zulu men usually got married when they were about 30 years old.

Guests at Zulu wedding ceremonies stood in a circle. They sang, cheered, and yelled to each other.

The king's kraal was the largest kraal in Zululand.

BECOMING A SOLDIER

A new group of soldiers began training every three or four years. Boys between 14 and 18 years old trained with local chiefs. These young men trained for two or three years. Then they were brought before the king to become a unit of the Zulu army. The units, called amabutho, were stationed on the king's homestead. A senior officer called an induna led the soldiers.

MILITARY KRAALS

Zulu soldiers lived in military kraals. The kraal was made up of huts for the soldiers to live in. The huts were arranged in a circle that was about I mile (1.6 kilometers) around.

A hedge of branches surrounded the ring of huts. Another hedge inside the ring separated the huts from the center of the circle. The king's cattle were in the middle of the circle. There was also room in the middle for the army units to gather.

For about six months, young Zulu soldiers lived and worked together. They kept the training grounds in good condition and herded the king's cattle. They also hunted animals for the king and acted as his police force.

The soldiers went home to their families after their six months of training. They returned to serve the king for a few months each year. They also returned in times of war.

CHAPTER III

DEADLY ZULU WEAPONS

LEARN ABOUT
- Spears and shields
- Regiments
- Dressing for war

*Zulu weapons were made by hand
from materials in the world around them.*

The Zulu made their weapons from the wood and rocks around them. They used two types of spears.

The main Zulu weapon was a stabbing spear called an iklwa. Warriors used the iklwa in hand-to-hand combat with their enemies. The blade was 14 to 18 inches (36 to 46 centimeters) long. It was sharp on both sides. The blade was placed on a shaft about 2.5 feet (.8 meters) long.

A warrior would thrust his iklwa into the enemy with an underhand motion and then rip it out. The Zulu warriors cried "uSuthu" when they stabbed their enemies. According to different translations, "uSuthu" can mean "kill" or "the Zulu royal house."

The Zulu throwing spear had a long handle and a small blade. It was about 3.5 feet (1.1 meters) long, including a blade that was 7 inches (18 centimeters) long.

Spear
Aside from battle, Zulu warriors used throwing spears to hunt for thousands of years.

Headdress
Each unit, or amabutho, had a different type of headdress.

Shield
Warriors made their shields to be about two-thirds their own height.

Bare feet
Going barefoot helped Zulu warriors move quickly through the tall grass.

SHIELDS, CLUBS, AND GUNS

Zulu warriors carried leather shields for protection in battle. The king gave cattle to each unit. Soldiers used the cattle to make leather for their war shields. When the nation was at peace, the king kept the shields. That way, his warriors could not rise up against him.

Each unit put its own pattern on the shields. Shields could be colored black or white and had black or white dashes on them. These patterns allowed warriors to tell each unit apart.

The Zulu also carried clubs called knobkerrie. Each club had a large round knob at the end. Warriors carved each knobkerrie from a single piece of hard wood.

Some Zulu warriors also carried guns. They stole them from enemies or got them through trade. But the Zulu were not trained to use guns. The Zulu also made their own bullets. These homemade bullets were not as powerful as European bullets. The Zulu's guns had little effect on their enemies.

GOING TO WAR

The Zulu dressed lightly for war to stay cool in the hot African climate. The king and other leaders wore the skins of rare animals like leopards. Other warriors wore headdresses of feathers and animal fur around their waists. Tufts of animal skin hung around their shins, ankles, and arms.

Some warriors also wore necklaces made of animal horns and wood. The necklaces meant the warrior had great skill in battle.

The main Zulu battle plan was called "the Beast's Horns." It used two groups of soldiers on the outside and one in the middle. The outside groups were called the horns. They surrounded the enemy first. Then the group in the middle, called the chest, attacked.

EDGE FACT

The British scattered broken bottles in front of their camps to slow down the barefoot Zulu warriors.

Zulus traveled barefoot. They toughened their feet by dancing on thorns.

CHAPTER II

DECLINE
OF THE
ZULU NATION

LEARN ABOUT
- An outmanned army
- Defeat
- Pride in their past

The British forces at the battle of Khambula far outnumbered the Zulu.

For nearly 40 years, the Zulu fought off small groups of Dutch and British colonists. In 1879, the fighting exploded into the Anglo-Zulu War. The Zulu warriors fought hard and launched organized attacks. They had some early successes. But eventually, the British overpowered them.

In the battle of Khambula, the Zulu used the Beast's Horns to surround the British. But British firepower proved to be too strong. As the Zulu fled from Khambula, the British followed and continued to attack. Many warriors were too tired to even lift their shields to defend themselves. Almost 800 warriors died at the battle site. Hundreds more were killed during the retreat. Many injured Zulu warriors died trying to make their way home. The Zulu did not have experience treating bullet wounds.

King Cetshwayo became king of
the Zulu people in 1872.

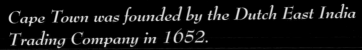

The Zulu fought bravely during the Anglo Zulu War.
But too many of the battles were lost. The Zulu did not
have enough warriors to protect their land. In August 1879,
the British captured King Cetshwayo. They held him in
Cape Town, South Africa, away from his people.

A BROKEN NATION

The Anglo-Zulu War crippled the Zulu nation. The
British soldiers burned Zulu homesteads and took their
cattle. The nation lost 10,000 men. There were fewer men
to raise cattle, hunt, and care for their families.

British soldiers destroyed Zulu homesteads, leaving the Zulu homeless.

After the war, the British took control of Zululand. The British government gave much of the land to white settlers. In 1887, Zululand became part of the British colony of Natal. It became part of the Union of South Africa in 1910.

A PROUD PEOPLE

The white government removed black South Africans from their land. They were forced to live in places called homelands.

Blacks and whites lived under an unfair system of laws called apartheid. Many blacks were killed or jailed under this system. Apartheid finally came to an end in 1991.

Today, 7 million Zulus live in South Africa. Laws now state that blacks and whites should be treated equally. Many Zulus live in the province of KwaZulu-Natal. Some have adopted a modern lifestyle and live in South Africa's bustling cities. Others still raise cattle and live the traditional Zulu way of life.

The Zulu now have a voice in South African government. The Zulu are very proud of their history and their nation. They continue to remember their past and celebrate the bravery of King Shaka and his warriors.

The Zulu people celebrate their past by performing traditional dances.

GLOSSARY

amabutho (ah-mah-BOO-thow) — the Zulu word for a unit of soldiers

apartheid (uh-PAR-tate) — the practice of keeping people of different races apart

conquer (KAHNG-kuhr) — to defeat and take control of an enemy

homestead (HOHM-sted) — a group of huts belonging to the same Zulu family

iklwa (IX-wah) — a Zulu stabbing spear

induna (in-DOO-nah) — a Zulu word meaning *headman*; an induna led each unit of Zulu soldiers.

knobkerrie (NAB-ker-ee) — a short wooden club with a ball at one end

province (PROV-uhnss) — a district or a region of some countries

READ MORE

Gleimius, Nita. *The Zulu of Africa.* First Peoples. Minneapolis: Lerner, 2003.

Graham, Ian. *South Africa.* Country File. North Mankato, Minn.: Smart Apple Media, 2005.

Spengler, Kremena. *South Africa: A Question and Answer Book.* Questions and Answers: Countries. Mankato, Minn.: Capstone Press, 2007.

INTERNET SITES

FactHound offers a safe, fun way to find Internet sites related to this book. All of the sites on FactHound have been researched by our staff.

Here's how:
1. Visit *www.facthound.com*
2. Choose your grade level.
3. Type in this book ID **1429613130** for age-appropriate sites. You may also browse subjects by clicking on letters, or by clicking on pictures and words.
4. Click on the **Fetch It** button.

FactHound will fetch the best sites for you!

INDEX